My Treasury of
Fairy Tales

Produced for Woolworths plc
242 Marylebone Road,
London, NW1 6JL

www.woolworths.co.uk

ISBN 978-1-4075-2737-6
Printed in China

My Treasury of
Fairy Tales

Retold by Ronne Randall
Illustrated by Anna C. Leplar

Contents

The Grimm Brothers

Cinderella

Once upon a time there was a pretty young girl who lived alone with her father, as, sadly, the girl's mother had died when she was a baby.

As the years passed, her father decided she needed a mother. So he got married again. The girl was excited, for her new stepmother had two daughters of her own, and she looked forward to having stepsisters.

But the stepmother was unkind, and the stepsisters were mean. The girl, who was a gentle, happy child, did her best to get along with them anyway.

Then, one day, the girl's stepmother said to her, "You must help to do the housework."

So every day, the girl got up at dawn to cook and clean and wash and sew for her stepmother and stepsisters. Soon the girl's pretty clothes were in rags and tatters, and she was not allowed any new ones.

Not long after, her stepmother said to the girl, "Since you spend so much time in the kitchen, you can sleep beside the fire."

So every night she curled up to sleep beside the fire. Soon her clothes and hair were so grey with ash and cinders that everyone called her Cinderella.

One morning, a messenger came to the house with a special invitation. There was to be a ball at the royal palace. All the young women in the kingdom were invited so that the young prince could choose a bride.

Cinderella's stepsisters were so excited. "We must look our best!" they cried.

"Cinderella! Comb my hair!" shouted one stepsister.

"Cinderella! Lace my dress!" ordered the other.

"Cinderella! Bring my jewels!"

"Cinderella! Fetch my shoes!"

When they were dressed, the two stepsisters admired themselves in the mirror. Cinderella looked on and sighed. She wished she could go to the ball, too.

As an elegant carriage took her stepsisters to the ball, Cinderella sat beside the hearth and wept.

"How I wish I could go to the ball," she cried.

Suddenly, a strange light filled the room.

"Dry your tears, my dear," said a gentle voice.

Cinderella looked up. A silvery glow surrounded a kind-looking woman with a glittering wand.

"Who are you?" asked Cinderella, blinking in wonder.

"I am your fairy godmother," she replied. "I have come to help you go to the ball."

"But how?" asked Cinderella.

"I will show you," said her fairy godmother, leading her out to the garden.

"Find me a big pumpkin, six white mice, six frogs and a rat," said the fairy godmother.

Cinderella found everything as quickly as she could.

The fairy godmother tapped the pumpkin with her wand. Before Cinderella's eyes, the pumpkin changed into a magnificent golden coach.

Next, the fairy godmother waved her wand over the six white mice. A shower of sparks lit the air, and suddenly, instead of mice, six prancing horses stood before Cinderella.

"Ohhh!" she breathed in delight.

Then, with a gentle tap of her wand, the fairy godmother changed the six frogs into handsome footmen dressed in green velvet jackets. One more tap, and the rat became a smart coachman.

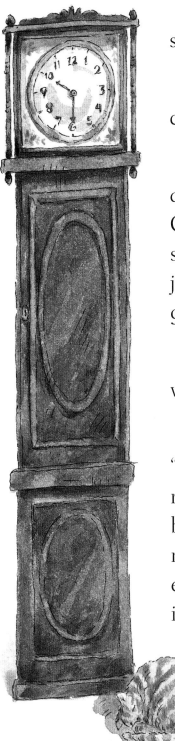

Cinderella was entranced. But still something was not right.

"But what about my ragged clothes?" she asked.

Her fairy godmother answered with a gentle tap of her wand. Instantly, Cinderella's dusty dress became a shimmering ball gown, twinkling with jewels. On her feet were two sparkling glass slippers.

"Thank you!" gasped Cinderella with delight.

"Now," said her fairy godmother, "you are ready for the ball. But, remember this: you must be home before midnight. At the stroke of midnight the magic will end, and everything will change back to what it was."

"I will remember," promised Cinderella as she stepped into the golden carriage.

When Cinderella arrived at the ball, everyone turned to look at her. No one knew who Cinderella was. Even her own stepsisters didn't recognize the beautiful girl in the dazzling gown.

But the prince thought that she was the loveliest, most enchanting girl he had ever seen. He never left her side, and danced only with her. Before the evening was over, he was in love with her.

Cinderella was falling in love with the prince, too. As she whirled round the room in his arms, Cinderella felt so happy that she forgot her fairy godmother's warning.

All at once, she heard the clock chime – once, twice, … twelve times!

"Oh!" cried Cinderella. "I must go!" And before the prince could stop her, she ran from the ballroom and out of the palace.

"Wait!" cried the prince, dashing after her. But by the time he reached the palace steps, the mysterious girl had disappeared. All he could see was a ragged kitchen maid hurrying towards the palace gates.

But then he saw something twinkling on the steps – a single glass slipper. The prince picked it up.

"This will help me find her!" he said.

The next morning, the prince made an announcement.

"I will marry the woman whose foot fits the glass slipper," he declared. "I will search the kingdom until I find her."

That very day, he began going from house to house, looking for his true love. Every young woman in the kingdom tried on the glass slipper, but it didn't fit anyone.

At last the prince came to Cinderella's house. Her stepsisters were waiting to try on the slipper.

The first stepsister pushed and squeezed, but she could barely get her fat toes into the tiny slipper.

The second stepsister's feet were even bigger. But she too tried to cram her foot into the dainty little shoe.

But it was no use.

The prince was turning to leave when a soft voice asked, "May I try the slipper, please?"

As Cinderella stepped forward to try on the slipper, her stepsisters began to laugh and make fun of her.

"Get back to the kitchen where you belong!" ordered her stepmother.

But the prince stepped forward.

"Everyone should have a chance," he said gently, "even a kitchen maid. Please," he said to Cinderella, "try on the slipper."

Cinderella sat down and took off her rough wooden clogs. The prince held out the sparkling slipper. And suddenly...!

Cinderella

"Oh!" gasped her stepsisters.

"Oh my!" choked her stepmother.

For, of course, Cinderella's dainty foot fitted into the slipper perfectly.

As her stepsisters gazed in amazement, the prince joyfully took Cinderella in his arms.

"You are my one true love," the prince said to Cinderella. "Will you be my bride?"

"Yes," said Cinderella, with shining eyes.

Her stepsisters and stepmother were still trembling with shock as they watched Cinderella ride off to the palace in the prince's own carriage.

Cinderella and the prince were soon married, and because Cinderella was good and kind, she invited her stepsisters and stepmother to the wedding. They were never unkind again, and Cinderella and the prince lived happily ever after.

The End

Hans Christian Andersen

The Ugly Duckling

One sunny summer day, a mother duck built her nest among the reeds near the moat of an old castle. There she laid her eggs, and there she sat, keeping them warm, day after day.

Finally, the eggs began to crack. Peep! Peep! Out popped each fuzzy little duckling's head, one after another.

Mother Duck nuzzled each of her babies.

"Welcome," she quacked.

Then she noticed that one last egg, the biggest one of all, had not yet hatched.

"Oh, dear!" she said, sitting down again. "I wonder how much longer this one will take!"

Finally, a long time later, the biggest egg began to crack.

"Honk! Honk!" said the duckling, tumbling out. He was much bigger and scruffier than the other ducklings.

"He's not as pretty as my other babies," Mother Duck said to herself. "But I'll look after him, just the same."

The next morning, Mother Duck took all her babies, even the big, ugly one, to the moat for their first swimming lesson.

They all followed her into the water, splish-splosh-splash, one by one. They all swam beautifully – and the big, ugly duckling swam best of all!

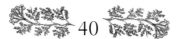

The Ugly Duckling

The other ducks came to watch.

"Who's that scruffy creature?" squawked one.

"He's my youngest duckling," said Mother Duck. "See how well he swims!"

"But he's so big, and so UGLY!" quacked the other ducks, laughing. While his brothers and sisters swam along, the little ugly duckling paddled into the reeds and tried to hide.

Mother Duck came over to him.

"Don't worry about those silly ducks," she told him. "I'll take you to the farmyard this afternoon. I'm sure the animals there will be kinder."

But she was wrong. As soon as the farmyard animals saw the ugly duckling, they began to laugh and shout.

"Most of your ducklings are lovely," clucked the hen. "But look at that big, scruffy, UGLY one! He's nothing like the others!"

"He's too ugly for this farmyard!" cackled the goose.

The pig snorted and said, "Why, he's the ugliest duckling I've ever seen!"

The little ugly duckling ran away and hung his head in shame.

The same thing happened the next day, and the day after that. The ducks on the moat and the animals in the farmyard all teased the ugly duckling, and chased him and called him names. Even his own brothers and sisters made fun of him and tried to peck him when they went swimming. The ugly duckling had no friends at all.

The ugly duckling was so sad and lonely that he decided to run away, out into the big, wide world. Early one morning, before anyone else was awake, he ran away, through the reeds, past the moat and the farmyard and the castle walls, till he came to a marsh.

There he saw a flock of wild ducks dabbling in the water.

"What kind of bird are you?" they asked.

"I'm a duckling," the ugly duckling replied.

"No, you're not," said the biggest duck. "You're much too ugly! We don't want to have anything to do with you!" And they turned away, leaving him alone.

The ugly duckling spent two lonely days on the marsh, far from the other ducks. Then, on the third day, a group of hunters came, scaring all the ducks away.

The frightened ugly duckling ran across the marsh and over fields and meadows. When he saw a cottage at the edge of the woods, he flew down and crawled in through a window, curled up in a corner of the kitchen and fell fast asleep.

An old woman lived in the cottage with her cat and her hen. The next morning, the cat and the hen found the ugly duckling.

"Can you lay eggs?" clucked the hen.

"No," said the ugly duckling.

"Can you catch mice?" meowed the cat.

"No," said the ugly duckling.

"Then you're useless!" said the cat.

"And you're VERY ugly!" added the hen.

"You'd better get out of here, before I scratch you!" hissed the cat.

So, once again, the ugly duckling ran away, out into the big, wide world.

The ugly duckling wandered far and wide until he came to a lake where he could swim and find food. There were other ducks there, but when they saw how ugly he was, they kept far away from him.

The ugly duckling stayed on the lake all summer. Then the autumn came, and the weather began to grow cold. All the other ducks began to fly south, where the weather was warmer. The ugly duckling shivered by himself in the tall grass beside the lake.

One evening, just before sunset, the ugly duckling looked up and saw a flock of big, beautiful birds above him. Their white feathers gleamed in the rosy-gold sunlight, and they had long, graceful necks. They were flying south, just like the ducks.

The ugly duckling flapped his stubby wings and stretched his neck to watch them for as long as he could. They were so beautiful that he felt like crying.

"I wish I could go with them," he thought. "But they would never even look at someone as ugly as I am."

Autumn turned to winter, and the lake froze solid. The ugly duckling couldn't swim any longer. His feathers were caked with ice and snow, and he couldn't find any food.

Luckily, a farmer found the ugly duckling and brought him home to his family. The farmer's wife warmed the ugly duckling up by the stove, and the farmer's children tried to play with him. But they were loud and rough, and the ugly duckling was frightened. He flapped his wings and knocked over a milk pail.

The children screamed and laughed, and tried to catch the ugly duckling, which only frightened him more. The ugly duckling flew across the kitchen – right into the flour bin! The farmer's wife chased him out of the house and into the yard, where he hid among some bushes.

Somehow, the ugly duckling found his way to a swamp, and there he managed to live for the rest of the long, hard winter.

At last spring came, bringing bright, warm sunshine. The ugly duckling spread his wings, and was amazed to find that they were big and strong. He flew up into the air and across the fields to a canal. There, swimming along the glassy water, he saw the beautiful birds he had seen last autumn.

"I'd better hide," he thought. "If they see me, they will just chase me and call me names like all the others have."

But when the birds saw him, they swam over to meet him.

"Hello!" they said.

The ugly duckling looked around. He couldn't believe they were talking to him!

"We are swans," explained one of the birds. "And so are you – you are a very fine young swan indeed!"

The ugly duckling looked down at his reflection in the water. It was true – a handsome swan looked back at him!

The other swans made a circle around him and nuzzled him with their beaks. "Welcome," they said. "We would be happy to have you in our flock!"

The new young swan thought his heart would burst.

"I never dreamed I could be so happy," he thought, "when I was a little ugly duckling."

And, looking around at his new friends, he knew that he would be happy forever.

The End

The Grimm Brothers

Little Red Riding Hood

There was once a little girl who lived with her mother at the edge of the forest. She was kind and sweet, and everyone loved her.

On the other side of the forest lived the little girl's granny. Granny looked forward to her granddaughter coming to visit, and always gave her a present.

The very best present was a riding cape, with a hood, made of red velvet. The little girl liked it so much that she wore it all the time. So everyone called her Little Red Riding Hood.

One day, Little Red Riding Hood's mother put some cake and fruit in a basket.

"These are for Granny," Mother told Little Red Riding Hood. "She isn't feeling well, and these goodies will cheer her up and help her get better."

"I'd like to help Granny get better!" said Little Red Riding Hood. "Can I take the goodies to her?"

"Of course," said Mother. "But you must promise to be very careful on your way through the forest. Stay on the path, and don't speak to ANY strangers!"

"I promise, Mother," said Little Red Riding Hood, and off she went.

As Little Red Riding Hood skipped along the path through the forest, she didn't know that a sly, greedy old wolf was watching her from behind a tree!

When she was just a little way down the path, the wolf sprang out in front of her.

"Good morning, my dear!" said the wolf, with a big, toothy grin.

Little Red Riding Hood remembered what her mother had told her, and she didn't speak to the wolf. She kept walking straight down the path. But that sly old wolf just followed her!

"I can see what a kind girl you are," said the wolf. "Won't you wish me a good morning?"

Now, Little Red Riding Hood was kind and sweet. So she stopped for just the tiniest moment and said, "Good morning, sir."

The sly old wolf smiled a very wide smile, thinking what a sweet, tasty snack Little Red Riding Hood would make. "Where are you going on this fine morning?" he asked.

Not wanting to be rude, Little Red Riding Hood answered, "To my granny's house, on the other side of the forest, sir. She isn't feeling well, and I'm taking some goodies to cheer her up."

"Hmm," the wolf thought to himself. "This little girl might make a sweet snack, but her granny would make a tasty meal!" He began to work out a crafty plan.

"Wouldn't your granny like some pretty flowers?" the wolf asked Little Red Riding Hood. "There are so many growing near the path!"

"Yes, Granny loves flowers," said Little Red Riding Hood. "A pretty posy would help cheer her up!"

Little Red Riding Hood began to gather the flowers growing near the path. But soon she forgot her mother's warning not to stray from the path. She strayed further and further into the forest, finding all the very prettiest flowers for Granny.

Meanwhile, the wolf hurried to the other side of the forest and went straight to Granny's house. He tap-tapped lightly on the door.

"Who's there?" called Granny.

"It's Little Red Riding Hood," called the wolf, in his softest, sweetest voice. "I've brought you a basket of goodies!"

"Just lift up the latch, open the door and come in," said Granny.

So the wolf lifted the latch … opened the door … and went right in.

Before poor Granny even knew that it was the wolf, he had gobbled her up in one big gulp.

Then he put on her nightcap and crept into her bed with the covers tucked under his chin.

"I'll have the little girl for dessert!" he said to himself with a big, toothy grin.

A little while later, Little Red Riding Hood arrived at the cottage with a pretty posy of flowers. She tap-tapped lightly on the door.

"Who's there?" called the wolf in his gentlest granny voice.

"It's Little Red Riding Hood," she replied. "I've brought you a basket of goodies!"

"Just lift up the latch, open the door and come in," said the wolf.

So Little Red Riding Hood lifted the latch, opened the door and went right in.

Little Red Riding Hood looked over at the bed.

"Poor Granny must be very ill," she thought. "She looks so strange!"

She stepped closer to the bed.

"Oh, Granny!" she gasped. "What big eyes you have!"

"All the better to see you with, my dear," said the wolf. Little Red Riding Hood stepped even closer.

"Oh, Granny!" she said. "What big ears you have!"

"All the better to hear you with, my dear," said the wolf. Little Red Riding Hood stepped right up to the bed.

"Oh, Granny, what big hands you have!"

"All the better to hold you with!" said the wolf.

"Oh, Granny!" she said. "What big teeth you have!"

"All the better to eat you with!" growled the wolf, jumping out of bed. And he gobbled up Little Red Riding Hood in one big gulp!

With his belly so full it was almost ready to burst, the wolf lay back down on the bed and fell fast asleep.

At that moment, a hunter was passing Granny's cottage, and he heard a strange sound coming through the open window.

"The poor old woman is snoring very loudly!" the hunter said to himself. "I'd better go in and see if she's all right."

So, in went the hunter. Of course he saw that it wasn't Granny who was snoring at all – it was the wolf!

"I have been hunting you for a long time," he cried. "Now, at last, I have found you!" He raised his gun to shoot the wolf. But then he looked at the wolf's belly.

"You sly old wolf!" cried the hunter. "From the size of your belly, I'd say you've swallowed poor old Granny!"

He took out his hunting knife and very carefully slit open the wolf's belly – zip, zip!

Out jumped Granny – and Little Red Riding Hood, too!

"Thank you for saving us!" said Granny.

"It was so dark and horrible in there!" said Little Red Riding Hood.

While the wolf was still asleep, Little Red Riding Hood went outside and got some stones. She brought them in and filled the wolf's belly with them. Then the hunter stitched up the wolf's belly as good as new.

When the wolf woke up a little while later, he had such a bellyache that he ran out of the cottage moaning and groaning. He went off to hide in a cave, and was never, ever seen again!

As soon as the wolf was gone, Little Red Riding Hood and Granny sat together to enjoy the basket of goodies. Before long, Granny was feeling much better.

Little Red Riding Hood said, "As long as I live, I will never leave the path and run off into the woods by myself if Mother tells me not to." And she never did.

The End

The Princess and the Pea

Hans Christian Andersen

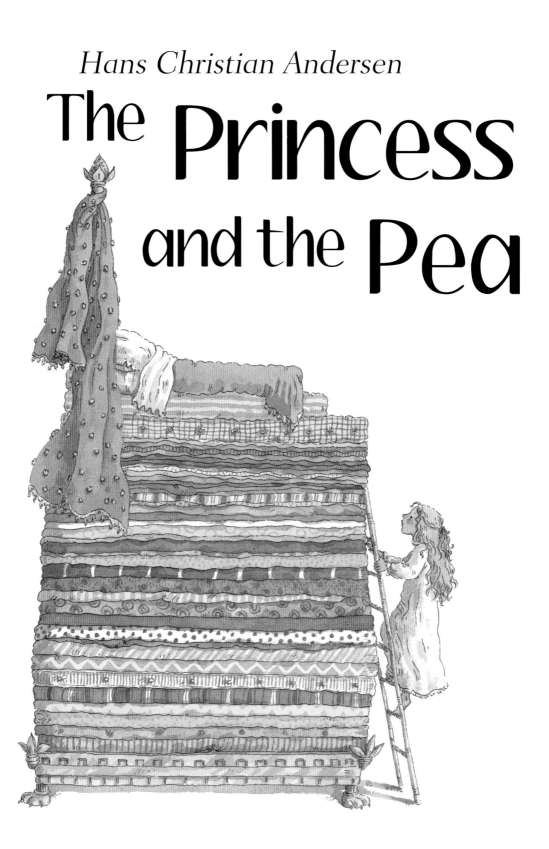

A long time ago, in a land far away, there lived a king and queen who had just one son. The prince was grown up and it was time for him to marry a princess.

"And she must be a *real* princess," the prince told the king and queen.

But there were no princesses in the land where he lived, so the king and queen arranged for the prince to travel to strange and distant lands to find a bride.

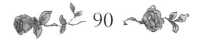

The prince travelled north through frozen lands, until he came to a castle where a princess lived.

This princess was tall and fair, with skin as soft as a peach. But when she laughed she sounded like a braying donkey! And though she was clever, she was also vain and boastful.

"Not only am I exquisitely beautiful," she told the prince, "but I can name every capital city of every country in the world and I can speak twenty-four languages! You will never meet anyone as clever as me!"

"A *real* princess would never be so boastful," thought the prince. "I can't marry her!"

So the prince travelled south through hot, sandy deserts, until he came to a palace where a princess lived.

This princess had long, gleaming hair the colour of midnight, and skin that smelled of sweet almonds. She also had the most enormous feet!

But though she was very beautiful, the princess would not speak to the prince. She would not even smile at him. She held her pretty nose high in the air.

"A *real* princess would never be so proud," thought the prince. "I can't marry her!"

And so the disappointed prince travelled east through misty lands and over windswept mountains, until he came to a mansion where a princess lived.

This princess was small and neat, with rippling red hair. She had a charming smile and a lovely voice – but she told the most shocking lies!

"Last night I ate a whole elephant for dinner," she told the prince. "It was as big as this room!"

"Really?" said the prince. "How amazing!"

"A *real* princess would never tell such shocking lies," thought the prince. "I can't marry her!"

A year had passed when the prince returned home from his travels, weary, sad and lonely.

"I will just have to remain a bachelor," he told the king and queen.

One evening, not long after the prince had come home, a terrible storm blew in from the west. Outside the window, lightning flashed and thunder rumbled, and rain washed down in sheets.

Inside the palace, the prince sat with the king and queen by the fireside, listening to the storm.

Suddenly, there was a knock at the castle door! The king was so surprised that he went to answer it himself.

There, standing in the windy doorway, was the most bedraggled young woman the king had ever seen.

Water ran down her hair and face, and her clothes were sopping wet and muddy. Water ran in through the toes of her shoes and out again through the heels.

"Good evening, Your Majesty," she said to the king, curtsying politely. "I am a princess, and I need shelter for the night. May I please come in?"

The king could hardly believe that this soggy, sorry-looking creature was a princess, but he invited her in anyway.

"Of course," he said. "Please come in out of the storm. "We will gladly give you shelter for the night."

When the king told the prince that a princess had turned up at the door, the prince was very eager to meet her. But the queen told him he would have to wait.

"The princess said that she couldn't possibly meet you wet and bedraggled," the queen explained. "She has gone to have a bath and change into some dry clothes."

"That's a good sign," said the prince. "But how can we be certain that she is a *real* princess?"

"I have an idea," said his mother. "Just leave everything to me." Off went the queen to the kitchen. She asked the cook for a single, tiny, dried pea.

A short while later, the princess arrived in the main hall dressed in the queen's clothes. Her hair shone, her cheeks were rosy, and her eyes sparkled merrily to match her smile. She certainly looked like a real princess.

The prince and princess sat beside the fire and talked for hours. The princess was clever, charming and seemed honest. The prince was enchanted – but he still wasn't sure that the princess was a *real* princess.

Meanwhile, the queen went to the best guest bedroom carrying a single, tiny, dried pea.

In the bedroom, she put the pea under the bed mattress. Then she asked a servant to bring another mattress to put on top of the first, and then another mattress, and another, and another…! At last there were TWENTY mattresses on the bed!

But even that wasn't enough. The queen told the servant to put twenty soft, cosy quilts on top of the twenty mattresses. Then she had a ladder brought for the princess.

As soon as the queen was satisfied that the bed was ready, she showed the sleepy princess to her room.

The princess was surprised when the queen brought her to the bedroom with its towering bed and tall ladder. But she didn't protest or complain. She thanked the queen and wished her good night.

The princess climbed the ladder to the very top of the pile of mattresses and quilts. Sighing contentedly, she settled down to sleep. But the princess did not sleep a wink. She tossed and turned all night.

By morning, the princess felt tired and weary. When she came down to breakfast, the prince, the king and the queen greeted her eagerly.

"Did you sleep well?" asked the queen.

"I'm afraid not," sighed the princess. "There was something small and hard in the bed, and no matter which way I tossed and turned, I still felt it. I'm dreadfully tired, for I hardly slept at all."

"I'm so sorry," said the queen. "But I'm delighted, too! For this proves that you are indeed a *real* princess! Only a *real* princess would feel a tiny pea under twenty mattresses and twenty quilts!"

The Princess and the Pea

The prince was overjoyed, for he had already fallen in love with the princess – and she had fallen in love with him. And so they were married.

They had a splendid wedding, and they invited all the royal families of all the kingdoms the prince had visited.

And what happened to the pea? It was put on a velvet cushion in a glass case, and sent to the museum, where it is still on display to this very day!

The End

The Grimm Brothers

Snow White and the Seven Dwarfs

One day, as snowflakes fell, a queen sat sewing by her window. Suddenly the needle pricked her finger, and three drops of blood fell onto the snow.

Gazing at the red blood on the white snow, the queen sighed, "I wish I had a child as white as snow, as red as blood, and as black as the wood of the window frame."

Months later, the queen gave birth to a beautiful little girl, who had skin as white as snow, cheeks as red as blood, and hair as black as ebony wood. She was called Snow White.

Sadly, the queen soon died. The king married again, and the new queen was beautiful but vain. Every day she stood before her magic mirror and asked:

"Mirror, mirror, on the wall,
Who is the fairest one of all?"

The mirror always replied:

"You, oh Queen, are fairest of all!"

But little Snow White grew more lovely with each passing year. At last the day came when the queen's magic mirror said:

*"You, oh Queen,
are fair, it's true.
But Snow White is
now fairer than you!"*

The queen was filled with jealous anger.

"No one can be more beautiful than I am!" she snarled.

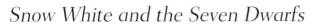

The queen summoned her huntsman.

"Take Snow White into the forest and kill her," said the wicked queen. "Bring me her heart in this chest."

So the huntsman took Snow White deep into the forest. He drew out his knife. But when he looked at Snow White he could not do it.

The huntsman killed a wild pig, put its heart in the chest and returned to the castle. The wicked queen was pleased, for she was sure that Snow White was dead.

Lost and alone, Snow White stumbled through the dark forest until she came to a little cottage. She knocked at the door, but there was no answer. She tried the latch – the door was unlocked, so she walked in.

Inside, she found a little table set with seven little plates of food and seven little cups of cordial. Snow White was hungry and thirsty. So she took a tiny bite from each plate and a tiny sip from each cup.

Soon, Snow White felt sleepy. She climbed the little ladder to the loft and found seven cosy little beds. She lay down on one of them and fell fast asleep.

The cottage belonged to seven dwarfs who worked in the gold mines. Imagine their surprise when they came home to find a stranger asleep in the cottage. And imagine Snow White's surprise when she awoke to find seven pairs of eyes staring at her!

When Snow White told the dwarfs her story, they felt sorry for her.

"If you cook and clean for us," they said, "you can stay here and we will look after you."

The next day, the dwarfs went to work in the mines. Snow White cooked and cleaned in the little cottage.

But back at the castle, the wicked queen was looking in her magic mirror. This time the mirror said:

*"Snow White is as lovely
    as she is good,
And she lives with the dwarfs,
    deep in the wood!"*

The queen was furious. She decided to kill Snow White herself. So she dressed up as a pedlar woman, and went to the dwarfs' cottage with a basket of ribbons.

"Pretty ribbons to buy!" she called.

Snow White saw the old pedlar woman and invited her into the cottage.

"Let me lace your dress with a pretty ribbon," said the pedlar woman. And she threaded a blue ribbon through Snow White's dress. Then she pulled it so tight that Snow White could not breathe and she fell down as if dead.

When the dwarfs came home that evening, they found Snow White lying pale and still on the floor. But when they untied the bodice lace, she began to breathe and her cheeks grew rosy once more.

"The queen will stop at nothing to hurt you," they told her. "You must not let anyone in!"

Snow White promised that she wouldn't.

The next morning, when the dwarfs left for the mine, they made sure that Snow White locked the door. She leaned out of the window to wave goodbye to them.

Back in the castle, the queen went to her magic mirror again. This time the mirror said:

"Fair Snow White, who lives in the wood,
Is still as lovely as she is good!"

Trembling with anger, the wicked queen made a magical potion. With the potion she poisoned a pretty hair comb. Then she set out for the dwarfs' cottage dressed as a poor peasant woman.

"Pretty combs to buy!" she cried.

Snow White opened her window. "I cannot let you in," she said.

"Then come outside and let me comb your beautiful hair," said the peasant woman, showing Snow White a beautiful jewelled comb. Snow White went outside. As the poisoned comb touched Snow White's beautiful black hair, she fell to the floor as if she were dead.

That night, when the dwarfs came home, they found Snow White lying in the cottage garden.

At first they were in despair, but then one of them noticed the comb.

"The evil queen has been up to her nasty tricks again!" said the eldest dwarf, kneeling down to look. Very gently, he took the comb out of Snow White's hair. She soon revived and her pale cheeks grew rosy again.

"The queen will stop at nothing to hurt you," the dwarfs told her. "You must not let anyone in and you must not go outside!"

Snow White promised that she wouldn't.

The next morning, when the dwarfs left for the mines, they made sure Snow White locked the door and they kept the key.

This time, when the queen's magic mirror told her that Snow White was still alive, she roared with fury.

The wicked queen made a magical potion. With the potion she poisoned one half of a rosy apple. Then she set off to the dwarfs' cottage dressed as an apple-seller.

"Sweet, rosy apples to buy!" she called outside the window. But Snow White remembered the dwarfs' warning.

"I cannot let you in and I cannot come out," she said.

"Where is the harm in a sweet, rosy apple?" asked the apple-seller. "Look, I will take a bite from this side. It is so sweet and juicy! Taste it for yourself."

Snow White took the poisoned apple. The moment she bit the poisoned apple, she fell down, lifeless.

When the dwarfs found Snow White lying on the floor again, they did everything they could to try to wake her. They loosened her laces, they combed her hair, they washed her face – but she was still and cold.

But the dwarfs did not have the heart to put poor Snow White in a cold grave. Instead, they made her a beautiful casket of glass. They wrote on it in gold letters that she was the daughter of a king.

They set the coffin amongst the grass and flowers outside their cottage. There they kept watch over her, day and night.

As time passed, Snow White remained as beautiful as ever. She looked as if she were sleeping peacefully in her glass coffin.

One day, a prince came riding through the forest.
When he saw Snow White, he instantly fell in love with
her. He begged the dwarfs to let him take the casket to
his palace.

At first the dwarfs would not agree, but the prince
pleaded with them.

"I will love her dearly forever," he promised, and at
last the dwarfs agreed.

As the dwarfs lifted the casket, they stumbled.
Suddenly a piece of poisoned apple fell from Snow
White's mouth and her eyes opened.

Snow White was alive!

Of course, the moment Snow White set eyes on the prince, she fell in love with him, and when he asked her to marry him, she happily agreed.

Everyone was invited to the wedding, including Snow White's stepmother. But when the wicked queen looked into her magic mirror, it said:

*"You, oh Queen,
are fair, it is true,
But there is one
still fairer than you.
The bride that the prince
will marry tonight
Is none other than the
lovely Snow White!"*

The wicked queen was so enraged that she fell down dead. And Snow White had nothing to fear ever again.

The End

Hans Christian Andersen

The Emperor's New Clothes

Once upon a time there was an emperor who loved new clothes. He loved clothes made of silk and velvet, and clothes made of satin and fur. He loved wool and taffeta and linen and lace. His tailors were busy making dozens of new garments every week.

Every morning, the emperor swept through the palace in brand-new clothes, enjoying the admiration of everyone he met.

"Your new ermine cloak is exquisite," his chief minister declared, bowing as the emperor passed.

"Indeed it is, Your Majesty," said the other ministers and courtiers, bowing in turn. They always said the same thing, no matter what they really thought. After all, no one wanted to upset the emperor!

One morning, the emperor told the chief minister to organize a grand parade to welcome some important foreign visitors.

"It will be a wonderful opportunity to show off a splendid new outfit!" said the emperor.

The emperor threw open his closet and gazed at the contents. After a moment, the emperor announced, "These clothes are all too ordinary! I want something EXTRAordinary. Something truly magnificent. Something no one has ever seen before! Find me the very best tailors and the very finest cloth in the kingdom!"

"Yes, Your Majesty," said the chief minister dutifully.

So the chief minister drew up a decree and messengers went to every corner of the land. The decree was read in every market square of every town.

"Hear ye! Hear ye!" the messenger proclaimed. "The emperor seeks the very finest, most talented, most gifted tailors in all the land. Anyone who can create a truly magnificent, extraordinary suit of clothes, unlike anything seen before, will receive a generous reward. Come to the palace next Thursday with samples of your cloth. Hear ye! Hear ye!"

Now, it just so happened that two rascals were in the crowd that had gathered in the marketplace to hear the decree. And they hatched a cunning plan.

On Thursday, a long line of tailors wound up to the palace doors. All of them had brought magnificent rolls of rich fabrics in brilliant colours.

But at the front of the line stood two tailors who seemed to have nothing at all.

"You shouldn't be here," said the chief minister. "The emperor only wishes to see tailors who have cloth to show him."

"We will leave if you insist," the two tailors said, "but we have been tailors to kings and princes all over the world. We have something very special to show the emperor, something no one has ever seen before."

Impressed, the chief minister ushered them into the palace.

The two tailors stood before the emperor, holding out their arms.

"This, Your Majesty," said the first man, "is the most amazing cloth in the world. It is so fine and delicate that it is almost invisible!"

"In fact," said his companion, "it IS invisible – but only to fools and simpletons. Anyone with wisdom and good sense can see how rare and beautiful it is."

Of course, the emperor could not see anything – because there was nothing there! The tailors were actually the two cunning cheats who had come to trick him.

Not wanting to look like a fool, the emperor said, "Yes, this cloth is magnificent. Don't you agree, chief minister?"

And the chief minister, who didn't want to look foolish either, said, "Yes, Your Majesty."

The emperor immediately ordered a new outfit made of the splendid cloth. All the other tailors were sent away, and a workshop was set up for the two cunning rascals. They asked for payment in advance, so the emperor gave them a purse filled with coins.

"First we have to weave more cloth," they told the emperor, "so we will need a loom and the finest gold thread in the kingdom."

When the loom and thread were brought, the two tailors got to work. Hiding the gold thread in their knapsacks, they began to 'weave'. But of course, the loom was empty!

The next day, the two tailors came to measure the emperor for his new outfit. One busied himself with the tape measure, while the other spoke to the chief minister.

"The emperor is such a fine figure of a man," said the first tailor, "that we will need even more cloth than we thought. We must have more money and more gold thread."

"Of course," said the chief minister, handing over another bulging purse.

"In this suit, you will look more handsome than ever before," the second tailor assured the emperor. "Your visitors will be amazed – unless, of course, they are fools and simpletons!"

"Of course," said the emperor, smiling nervously.

The Emperor's New Clothes

For the next few days and nights, the two rascals stayed in their workshop, keeping the doors locked.

As the day of the parade drew near, the emperor began to grow anxious.

"Go and see what the tailors are doing," he told his chief minister.

The two cunning rascals refused to let the chief minister in.

"It will spoil the surprise," they told him. "But if you give us more money, we can finish the suit sooner."

The chief minister handed over another purse filled with coins, then went back to the emperor.

"The new suit is beautiful," he told the emperor. "I am sure you will be pleased!"

The day of the parade arrived, and the tailors were summoned.

"Your new suit is ready!" they told the emperor proudly. "Here it is!"

As the emperor undressed, the tailors pretended to hand him his new clothes. And the emperor carefully pretended to put them on.

He pretended to step into the trousers …

… and he pretended to fasten them at the waist.

He pretended to put his arms in the sleeves of the tunic …

… and then he pretended to button all the buttons.

Finally, the two rascals pretended to tie the cloak around the emperor's shoulders, and to straighten the long train.

As the emperor strode proudly through the palace corridors, the palace courtiers and servants bowed and murmured words of praise.

The important foreign visitors were shocked to see the emperor wearing nothing but his wig and crown. And though they raised their eyebrows, nothing was said. No one would admit that they could not see the magnificent new suit of clothes. They all knew that the clothes were only invisible to fools and simpletons, and no one wanted to be thought a fool!

The Emperor's New Clothes

A huge crowd gathered to watch the grand parade. Everyone wanted to know if their friends and neighbours were simple fools who couldn't see the emperor's new clothes.

At last the royal procession came into view. The important foreign visitors walked in front, followed by the emperor's most important ministers.

Finally, a fanfare of trumpets announced that the emperor was coming.

A gasp rose from the crowd – but it was quickly followed by cheers.

"Look at the emperor's magnificent new clothes!" people cried. "Look at the fine cloth! Look at the colours!"

At the back of the crowd, one little boy hopped up and down see the emperor's magnificent new clothes.

Finally, the little boy pushed his way to the front of the crowd.

"The emperor has no clothes on!" he cried, pointing and laughing. The crowd fell silent. Then someone called out, "The boy is right! It's true – the emperor has no clothes on!"

Soon everyone in the crowd was saying it: "The emperor has no clothes on! The emperor has no clothes on!"

The emperor knew that they were right. He blushed with embarrassment. "I didn't want anyone to think I was a fool," he thought, "but I have turned out to be the biggest fool of all."

And so the emperor just kept walking stiffly, staring straight ahead. He never even saw the two cunning rascals sneak away, laughing and clutching their bags of gold.

The End

Hans Christian Andersen

Hans Christian Andersen was born in 1805 in Odense, Denmark. He was the son of a poor shoemaker. His father died when he was just eleven years old. So he became apprenticed to a weaver and tailor.

He ran away to Copenhagen when he was fourteen years old, where he worked in the theatre acting, dancing and singing.

While he was there, he became friendly with one of the directors of the theatre who sent him to school. In 1828, Hans went to the University of Copenhagen to study.

He later travelled around Europe and wrote many travel essays, plays and novels as well as over one hundred fairytales. His collection of *Fairy Tales and Stories* was published in 1837.

He died in 1875 aged seventy. There is now a Hans Christian Andersen museum in his home town of Odense.

The Grimm Brothers

Jacob Ludwig Carl Grimm, born in 1785, was just one year older than his brother Wilhelm Carl Grimm.

They were born in Hanau in Germany, but later moved to Kassel to live with an aunt so that they could attend a secondary school.

When their mother died in 1808, Jacob and Wilhelm went to work in a library to support their brothers and sisters. Both brothers went on to study law at the University of Marburg.

They published their first book in 1812, which was called *Children's and Household Tales*. Wilhelm later married Henriette Wild, who helped the brothers collect over two hundred traditional folktales.

Both brothers became professors at the University of Berlin and published many more books in their lifetime. Wilhelm died in 1859 and Jacob in 1863.